S0-BZD-720

DEEP FREEZE

KRISTIN F. JOHNSON

MINNEAPOLIS

Copyright © 2017 by Lerner Publishing Group, Inc.

All rights reserved. International copyright secured. No part of this book may be reproduced, stored in a retrieval system, or transmitted in any form or by any means—electronic, mechanical, photocopying, recording, or otherwise—without the prior written permission of Lerner Publishing Group, Inc., except for the inclusion of brief quotations in an acknowledged review.

Darby Creek
A division of Lerner Publishing Group, Inc.
241 First Avenue North
Minneapolis, MN 55401 USA

For reading levels and more information, look up this title at www.lernerbooks.com.

Front cover: © JonikFoto.pl/Shutterstock.com, snowy road scenery; © mycteria/Shutterstock.com, swirling snow; © iStockphoto.com/stanley45, man; © iStockphoto.com/robertiez, snowy trees scenery; © iStockphoto.com/Emily Skeels, dog, © iStockphoto.com/Marina Mariya (swirl).

Images in this book used with the permission of: © JonikFoto.pl/Shutterstock.com, snowy road scenery; © mycteria/Shutterstock.com, swirling snow; © iStockphoto.com/stanley45, man; © iStockphoto.com/robertiez, snowy trees scenery; © iStockphoto.com/Emily Skeels, dog, © iStockphoto.com/Marina Mariya (swirl).

Main body text set in Janson Text LT Std 12/17.5.
Typeface provided by Adobe Systems.

Library of Congress Cataloging-in-Publication Data

Names: Johnson, Kristin F., 1968- author.
Title: Deep freeze / Kristin F. Johnson.
Description: Minneapolis : Darby Creek, [2017] | Series: Day of disaster | Summary: "What is supposed to be a fun ice-fishing trip may turn deadly. When a boy arrives at a northern cabin during the blizzard of the century, he faces more than just frostbite"— Provided by publisher.
Identifiers: LCCN 2016018123 (print) | LCCN 2016034212 (ebook) | ISBN 9781512427769 (lb : alk. paper) | ISBN 9781512430929 (pb : alk. paper) | ISBN 9781512427837 (eb pdf)
Subjects: | CYAC: Blizzards—Fiction. | Survival—Fiction. | Minnesota—Fiction.
Classification: LCC PZ7.1.J624 De 2017 (print) | LCC PZ7.1.J624 (ebook) | DDC [Fic]—dc23

LC record available at https://lccn.loc.gov/2016018123

Manufactured in the United States of America
1-41501-23362-8/1/2016

For Ben N. and Ben V., "The Bens"

The day of the disaster, it was twenty degrees below zero, with snow that showed no sign of letting up.

Most of Zach's friends had left for warm spring break vacations, while Zach and his dad decided they would go ice fishing. A beach vacation was sounding much more appealing considering the way this trip was starting off. The temperature was dropping by the minute, and Zach was more likely to get frostbite than a suntan. This place was almost in Canada and it was freezing! No palm trees or sand here. All he could see from the window of his little cabin was blowing snow.

Zach balled his freezing hands into fists and saw by the glowing red numbers on his watch that his dad was over two hours late.

Normally, they would have driven up together, but Zach's dad was out of town on a work trip, so they had decided they would drive separately and meet at the cabin. Zach had planned to open up the cabin, get groceries, and have everything all set by the time his dad arrived. But when the snow started coming down harder, Zach skipped the grocery store and headed straight to the cabin to get the heater going. He wasn't hungry at the time, having just polished off a bag of tortilla chips on the drive up, but by now his stomach was growling. He wished his dad would show up so they could go get some food.

Zach walked over to the fridge to check if there was anything to eat. But even as he pulled open the handle he knew it was probably no use.

Empty. His dad was always meticulous about clearing any food out of the fridge before they left.

Zach shut the door and stared at the pictures stuck haphazardly to the fridge. He saw a scattered timeline of his life. An old picture of Zach missing his two front teeth from the Boy Scout trip where he had first learned how to fish. A wrinkled copy of Zach's freshman year football picture. A shot of him sitting behind the wheel of the old, tan family car right after he had gotten his driver's license. A picture of him in the dorky uniform he wore to his first job. All of these achievements had been followed quickly by a father-son trip up to the cabin to celebrate with a weekend of fishing.

They had planned this ice-fishing trip as soon as Zach got his college acceptance letter. It was supposed to be a last hurrah before Zach went away to college next year. He wouldn't have been surprised if his dad brought up a copy of the acceptance letter to stick on the fridge next to the picture with his childish, toothless smile.

Nothing had ever stopped them from celebrating with a fishing trip, so when his dad had called and said the weather forecasters predicted a blizzard, Zach insisted they go on the trip as planned. They had been there in storms before. Why should this one be a big deal?

There was a scratch on the cabin door.

"I'm coming. I'm coming!"

Zach opened the door and shivered as the cold hit him. Normally, he sweated through anything more than a t-shirt, but this storm was brutal. He was glad that he had put on a second pair of pants. He thought briefly about going out to the car to grab the spare sweatshirt he kept in the trunk, but decided he'd just wait until his dad showed up.

Skye, Zach's dog, bounded past him into the cabin. Her fur was covered in a layer of snow. She sneezed and shook out her fur, the same way she shook off after having a bath. Snow sprinkled all over the entry to the cabin. She nudged his hands. Her wet, snowy fur was freezing against his already numb fingers.

"Skye, you look more like a white husky than a golden retriever," Zach said as he dodged the spray.

Skye had loved coming up to the cabin ever since she was a puppy. She loved being outdoors and riding on the boat with them. His dad had said that since Skye was getting older, maybe she should sit this trip out. But as Zach was loading up the car with his fishing supplies, Skye hopped into the back seat. He took it as a sign that he should bring her.

"I hope Dad gets here soon," Zach thought aloud. What was taking him so long? The cabin was lonely without all three of them there together. Zach was glad he had brought Skye along.

Zach shivered. He thought he had turned the heat on as soon as he got to the cabin, but it didn't seem any warmer than when he arrived. He crossed the cabin and knelt down to check the knob next to the baseboard. He rapped his knuckles on the metal. The whole unit was ice cold. He turned the knob, but there was no satisfying *hiiissssss* telling him the heat had been adjusted or even turned on. He knocked his fist against the side of the heater. The heater started clanking but didn't seem to be heating up. Skye wandered over and stood over Zach's shoulder, breathing warm air into his ear.

Zach laughed. "Skye, you need a mint."

He held his hands over the heater vent. Still nothing. He stood up and looked around the room.

The old cabin had electrical heaters running along the baseboards. The small space had a combined living room and kitchen that held an outdated stove and a refrigerator with a broken handle. Everything inside the cabin was old and breaking down, including the heater.

Zach's dad had often made small adjustments in the heater to get things going again. Maybe it just needed some tightening up.

Zach grabbed the toolbox they kept by the cabin door and lugged it over to the heater. He dug through it until he felt the flathead screwdriver. Then he tightened the screws on the side of the heater's base. The clanking stopped, but the metal was still cold.

Skye pawed at the heater and looked intently at Zach.

"It's okay, Skye. I'll get it going," he said.

Zach remembered that his dad sometimes lit the pilot light again. He peeked into the heater's opening. Sure enough, the flame had gone out. He dug around the kitchen drawer and found an old book of matches alongside some mouse droppings. He made his way back to the heater, knelt down, and struck a match. But the flame blew out right away. Zach sighed, striking a second match. The old heater banged and clanked. It hissed and rattled, then started shaking.

Skye barked at the heater, the way she always barked at the vacuum cleaner back home—as if it was an intruder.

"It's going to be fine," Zach said, although even *he* had to admit that the heater did sound menacing. Zach stuffed the matches in his jeans pocket. He took a step away from the old heater, but in the tiny cabin there was really nowhere else to go. Then another noise began. Somewhere inside its belly, the heater groaned.

2

The heater actually groaned. Followed by a bang and a few pops. It was getting louder and shaking harder all the while.

Skye barked again and paced back and forth in front of the heater.

"Quiet!" Zach tried to calm the dog, but Skye ignored him. Zach didn't like being alone in the secluded cabin with a noisy heater and now a barking dog. The cabin was the only place around for seven or eight miles in any direction. But the noise in the cabin was not part of the peaceful vacation he had in mind.

Outside, snowflakes fell faster than they had only moments ago. His little tan car was completely covered by a layer of white, making it nearly unrecognizable. How could that have happened so quickly? He would have to dig the car out to get anywhere.

Zach pushed on the front door, but the spring at the top of the door creaked and stayed put.

Zach murmured to himself and kicked the door. The cabin door always got stuck at the worst times. Just like everything else in the cabin, it needed replacing.

The heater clanked again.

Zach really wanted to get away from the noise, but how was he going to stay warm if he left the cabin?

They used to build fires in the pit outside, but that was covered in snow. With all that snow falling, making a fire outside—or even finding dry wood—would be a challenge.

Meanwhile, the heater seemed to be getting worse. The sounds grew louder.

Skye nuzzled Zach's leg and yipped.

"Let me think," Zach said, rubbing her head, trying to calm her.

The heater gasped and knocked.

Skye growled low and erupted into barking, louder this time, more insistent.

The heater rumbled and shook some more. Steam rose from the top. Zach knew that he *really* needed to leave the cabin.

He grabbed his jacket, hat, and gloves. Zach glanced at the heater and dashed into the kitchen, throwing open the cupboards. Two cans of beans and a candy bar. He grabbed the stash and raced to the door.

The noise in the cabin was unbearable. A mixture of metal rattling and dog barking echoed off the walls.

Zach pushed on the cabin door again, but it still wouldn't budge. He kicked the bottom corner of it with the toe of his hiking boot, trying to loosen the stuck coil. After a few tries, the door started to wiggle. Zach shoved it open enough to squeeze out and slipped through the crack. Skye followed.

Just as they emerged into the cold, there was a loud crack and a sudden wave of heat. The heater blew up behind them.

3

Zach flew face first into the snow. For a moment, he lay stunned. What happened? An explosion. The heater. He rolled over and patted down his arms and legs. "I'm okay," he told himself, with his heart hammering. "I'm okay." Then, he looked around.

"Skye! Skye!"

The dog was cowering in the snow, surrounded by scraps of wood and metal. The explosion had shaken her up and she didn't want to move.

"Skye? Come here. What's wrong?"

She tucked her front paw up to her chest and started limping hesitantly toward Zach.

Just then, a glimmer of light in the snow caught his eyes. Zach surveyed the wreckage from the heater. The cabin windows were blown out. Broken glass stuck out of the snow everywhere, half hidden by the freshly-fallen powder.

"Skye! Wait! Don't walk through there."

Skye stopped. She whimpered and shook the injured paw she held out of the snow.

Zach walked over to her using wide steps, as if he were navigating a minefield. When he reached Skye, he knelt down and lifted her paw. She flinched the moment he touched her.

"It's okay, Skye." Zach turned Skye's paw as much as he dared so he could examine the pads on the bottom. A small tear cut the larger pad. A sliver of glass poked out of the edge of the wound. He tried to grab the glass to pull it out, but Skype yelped and wrenched her paw back out of his hand.

"It's okay, girl," Zach said to Skye. He stroked her head and slowly reached for her paw again. Once her paw was back in his hand, Zach knew that he would probably only get one more chance to get the glass out without risking it getting lodged in any deeper.

"Let's try one more time." He took a deep breath and lifted her paw a little bit higher, being as careful as possible. He turned it over and looked for the shard. When he found it again, he grabbed firmly and pulled. This time the glass came out. Skye licked his face and tenderly put her paw down into the snow.

Zach laughed, relieved. "You're welcome." But his hands were so cold. He grabbed his gloves that were sticking out of the snow next to him and pulled them on. He needed to get moving if he wanted to stay warm.

Zach shepherded Skye away from the worst of the wreckage, being careful to avoid any of the glass half-hidden in the snow. She left a red trail in the snow behind her where her injured paw touched the white ground, but she didn't seem to be too hurt. At least she was putting her paw on the ground again.

Zach looked around for the few things he had managed to gather from the cabin before the explosion. They had scattered throughout the yard when the heater blew. He shook off the snow and put on his jacket, then grabbed his hat and jammed it down over his ears. Other than the cans of beans and the candy bar that lay a few feet from him, nothing else seemed to survive the blast.

They needed help.

He pulled out his phone to call 9-1-1. His dad had cell service installed at the cabin a couple of years ago so he wouldn't miss any work calls. Normally Zach hated that his dad could be interrupted on their trips and liked that the service was still pretty shoddy. But now he was praying the call would go through. He checked his cell phone. One bar. He dialed the police. The call dropped even before he heard it ring. No signal. He tried texting his mom, but the message wouldn't send.

"Well, I guess we'll have to drive out of here. Ready to do some digging, Skye?" Zach said as he turned to look at the retriever. She was already turning white from the snow accumulating on her fur.

Zach made his way to the car. By now, the layer of snow was over a foot thick. He used his sleeve to push most of the snow off the driver's side door and reached into the car to grab the brush from under the driver's seat. Then he got to work clearing off the rest of the car.

The fallen snow came up to his mid-calf and fell into his hiking boots. The snow was getting heavier now. It wasn't melting on his jacket anymore—it was accumulating.

Snow and wind struck his face.

Skye trailed behind him and barked. She tried jumping through the snow, but she kept stopping to lick her injured paw.

"We can't stay out here! We'll freeze to death," Zach told her, but his voice was lost, sucked into the blowing wind.

Woof! Skye barked once more with finality.

Why was Skye so adamant? Maybe she was warning him about something, but Zach looked around and didn't see any danger.

A sound like a tree branch snapping in half came shooting out from the nearby woods. What was that? An animal knocking something over? A moose or bison? Or a bear?

He peered through the woods, but all he saw was a thick layer of white. Maybe he was just jumpy, but Zach thought he heard another snap coming from the direction of the trees.

4

Zach stood still, but he didn't hear anything else. He hoped it wasn't a bear.

Bearclaw Lake got its name because of the black bears that lived around the lake's edge. Zach tried to remember what he had learned about black bears in Boy Scouts. If he saw a black bear, the best thing to do was to make noise. Yeah, that's right. It was all coming back to him. If he ran, the bear would probably chase him. Plus, they can climb trees, so it wasn't like he could just climb his way to safety.

Zach had never been face-to-face with a bear before. And he hoped he never would be. The taxidermy black bear at the outfitter in town had towered over Zach as a kid and was still at least a foot taller than him.

He pulled up his sheepskin gloves a little further. He wanted to clear the car off before more snow accumulated. And before any animals decided they were hungry for a late lunch.

The brush cut through the snow, but he had to make several passes to clear the deep build-up. Even working fast, Zach struggled to keep up with the snow that was now persistently falling. It was falling almost faster than he could clear it off.

Zach needed to dig out the tires, too, or he'd never get anywhere. As he got around to the last tire, he looked up to see Skye leaping through the snow, trying to catch the falling flakes in her mouth.

She barked and shook new snow off her golden coat.

"Skye! Here, Skye!"

Skye's ears perked up. She was on alert. Her tags jingled as she jumped through the deep snow and over to Zach.

A few feet before she reached him, Skye tumbled through the snow in front of the trunk of the car. Zach rushed over to the dog, worried she may have hurt herself again, but was met with a reassuring bark. She had just tripped over a branch hidden in the fallen snow. Zach stroked Skye's back and looked at the car. He hadn't thought to look in the trunk. Maybe there was something in there that could be helpful.

He popped it open. The first thing that caught his eye was his sweatshirt and the fleece blanket his mom had made his freshman season of football. They would keep him warm, but the other items looked so useless now: fishing line, lures, rod, pliers to cut fishing line, cribbage board and cards, a pocket knife, a fishing guidebook, tarp, rope, and bungee cords. He took all of the supplies and shoved them in the back seat. Something tumbled out of the pile as he moved everything over. Zach scooped a spray bottle out of the snow and brushed it off. He almost laughed at the label: bear spray.

When Zach was younger, they had gone on a family trip to Yellowstone. The last service station they hit before driving into the main park sold bear spray. The picture on the display showed a totally freaked-out guy with a torn shirt, claw marks on his face, and blood running down his neck. Zach's dad said they were just trying to scare people into spending $40 for no reason, but his mom had still bought a bottle and stuffed it in their trunk. Zach sided with his dad during that particular argument, but now he was grateful his mom had been cautious. He looked around, as if a bear would come bolting out of the woods that very second. Zach shook his head—he was just being paranoid. He threw the bottle in the back seat with everything else.

Zach slammed the door closed and turned around. He squinted and shielded his eyes. The sun reflecting off the white everywhere was blinding. The edge of the road was harder to see, except for the outline of trees lining the road.

Zach looked at his watch. Four o'clock. Four already? Two more hours had gone by.

Zach's dad had never been this late before. It would be harder to see where he was going in the dark, especially with the snow blanketing everything.

What if something had happened to his dad on the way up? That curve on the main road got slippery in the winter, and with the drifting snow, driving conditions were horrible. His dad could have driven into a ditch. He could have braked and swerved to avoid hitting a deer. Maybe he had left Zach a message calling the trip off. Zach pulled the phone out of his pocket. Still no signal. Even if his dad had left a message, Zach wouldn't be able to get it. He needed to find his dad.

5

Zach encouraged Skye into the car and slid into the driver's seat. He reached his keys toward the ignition, but they fell out of his shaking hands before he could get the car started. His hands were so cold already. If he could drive back to the main road, he could get back into town—to food and to a warm fireplace.

He took off his gloves and fished around the floor mat for the keys. He remembered he once dropped a lure into the water of his ice-fishing hole and had to quickly grab at the freezing cold water to retrieve the lure. But now his hands were like ice and fishing around for the keys was even harder because his hands were already numbing before he even started the search. Finally, his fingers grasped the cold keys and pulled them up carefully like one of those crane games in the arcade that promised an expensive watch or wallet, but this time his keys were the prize.

Zach sat up in the seat again. He pushed the cold key into the ignition. He turned the key. Nothing. He tried again, giving it some gas. A sputter. Then nothing. Zach rushed out of the car and ran to the back with Skye at his heels. The tailpipe was completely covered in snow. He dug around it with his gloved hands, stopping every few seconds to shake out his hands. The prickly feeling washed through them, the pins and needles. He could not get frostbite. He needed to get the car heater going to warm up his hands.

Once he cleared the tailpipe, he climbed back in the car.

"Here, Skye." Zach motioned Skye closer and held the door for her to jump in the car.

Skye sat down in the passenger's seat as Zach dropped back into the driver's seat and slammed the door. He was tired from not eating. The chips he had brought with him for the drive were long gone and the crumpled bag at Skye's feet taunted him. Some neighbors back home said that up at their cabin, about twenty miles away from Zach's, they saw three black bears once outside of their place eating a bag of corn chips that had been left out. It was important not to leave food lying around because bears had such a good sense of smell and the food might attract them. Zach laughed to himself. He hardly had any food. Was it still enough to attract a bear?

He turned the key again, revving the engine several times. He revved again. Finally, the engine turned over. He let out a deep sigh. He pumped the gas pedal a few more times. His hands prickled and throbbed. He slapped them against his legs, trying to feel them again. He shoved them under his arms, anything to warm them up. The prickles shot through his fingers until the numbing lessened. He blew on them, but even his breath was cool. Zach shivered. The wind howled around the outside of the car, and the little car heater could only do so much.

Skye leaned into him, as if she knew her duty now was to warm Zach up. Or maybe she needed comforting. Zach ran his thumb along the fur between Skye's eyes.

"Good girl." Zach scratched Skye's wet ears. The dog panted quietly and leaned into the rub.

Zach's stomach growled again. He needed to eat before he could think of doing anything else. The candy bar? No. Save it. He eyed the two cans of beans. Beans. Perfect. One for now, one for later.

He pulled the pocketknife out of the pile of supplies from the trunk. It was one with tons of tools. He was sure it had—ah, yes, a can opener. Well, not exactly a can opener. More of a knife you had to work around the can to cut the lid off. He would have to remove his gloves to use the opener tool, so he wanted to be efficient about it. He couldn't afford to have his skin exposed to the cold any more than necessary, even though he was inside the car.

Zach took off his gloves and quickly fit the opener onto the cover of the can. He had never used that tool before, but he thought he could figure it out. He pressed down and pushed the blade forward. Repeat. Press down, push forward, repeat. He was halfway around the can when his hand slipped and the blade sliced right across his thumb.

Zach yelped in pain.

He pressed down on the finger right where he had cut it. Bright red blood gushed out.

6

He grabbed part of his "I'd rather be fishing" shirt, cut a strip off the bottom using his pocketknife, and held that in place over the wound. When he lifted the cloth, the cut was still oozing blood. Skye stood up in the passenger seat and whined.

"It's okay, Skye. I'll be fine. I just need to get the bleeding to stop."

He quickly pressed the cloth over the cut again and held his arm up in the air. He counted to sixty and looked at it again. The bone wasn't visible, so that was good. The bleeding hadn't stopped but it might have slowed a bit, so he covered it up again and held the cloth in place by making a fist.

Skye watched intently as, one handed, Zach whipped open the glove compartment and dug around with his good hand. No first aid kit. He kicked himself for not making sure the car had one. He closed the compartment and tightened the cloth around his hand for a makeshift bandage and pressed against it until the pain dissipated. Skye gave one last whimper and lay back down on the seat.

Zach looked at the beans again. The can was only half open. He carefully took the pocket knife and finished opening it. Pressing down was harder now, with his hand throbbing and a bulky cloth getting in his way. But hunger won out and he pressed on.

He wished he could heat the can over a fire, but there was no place to make a fire. He ate them right out of the can—careful not to cut himself on the jagged edge. Cold beans. Better than nothing.

Skye sat up again and started sniffing the can. She nudged her nose against the can and against his hand, bumping the sticky fingers he was eating the beans with.

"Okay. Just a second." Zach grabbed the discarded chip bag and dished some beans out for Skye, who lapped them up gratefully off the glossy, plastic bag.

After Zach finished his beans, he got out and cleared the windows one last time. Putting on his gloves was harder now since he had to work around the makeshift bandage, but he pulled them on all the same. He looked at the cabin again. Snow had drifted through the broken windows. Zach rubbed his face with his gloved hands. His cheeks were cold and numb in places. He had never had frostbite before but he was almost certain he was getting it now. They couldn't stay here. If they stayed, they could die.

When Zach got back in the car, Skye tried to jump out of the car, but Zach held her back.

"We don't have a choice," Zach said. "We have to go."

The snow was still coming down, but he thought he could see enough of the path to get through the gravel back roads and out to the main highway. Zach shifted the car into drive. It couldn't plow through snow like his friend's SUV, but at least it had front wheel drive.

The thick snow had drifted into big piles on the driveway, but Zach was pretty sure he could get through it if he tried. He had shoveled out the tires again as best he could with his one good hand, but he would never be able to clear off the rest of the driveway. If he could just get the wheels going he would try and push right through the other snowdrifts. Maybe they had even plowed the main road by now. His family's cabin was just over ten miles from a popular resort, so they would want to clear things out for anyone who had come here on vacation.

Zach had never driven with only one hand, but he was doing pretty well considering the other hand was bandaged and out of commission. His little car was doing pretty well too.

"I think we're going to make it, Skye," Zach said, looking over as she wagged her tail.

They had passed the first few landmarks: the end of the driveway, the clump of birch trees, the point where the road grew wider then went narrow again. He went around the final corner, but the road was slick with ice. He drifted right and whipped the steering wheel in the opposite direction. Zach tried to brake, but by now he couldn't stop the car from spinning out. By the time it stopped, he was facing the opposite direction and stuck in a thick pile of snow in the middle of the road.

Zach's arms shook. He had never lost control of his car before. He took a deep breath. The car was still in drive. He pressed on the gas. For a second, the car lunged forward, but it stopped after only a couple of feet.

"Come on!" Zach yelled at the car.

Skye barked once.

"Come *on*." Zach shifted the car into reverse and backed up a couple of feet.

Skye stood up and sat down again nervously in the passenger seat.

"I'll get us out, Skye. Don't worry."

He shifted into drive and pressed the gas. The car went forward a couple of feet, but stopped again. The wheels spun.

Zach yelled and hit the steering wheel with his good hand. He pressed on the gas again. The tires spun forward. Maybe he should just back up and try again. He put the car in reverse. But now the tires just spun in reverse.

"No!" He smacked the steering wheel three more times.

Meanwhile, snow pelted the windows. It was getting stickier and thicker. Flakes were falling in big pellets now. The wipers left icy streaks on the windshield. This was sleet. And he couldn't move the car at all.

1

The walk to the main road from here was about a mile. He knew that because he had often walked that way when he was visiting during the summer and sharing the cramped cabin with his family. In good weather, he could walk it in fifteen or twenty minutes. Today, it might take twice as long, fighting against the wind and slogging through the deep snow. And it was starting to get darker.

Zach looked down at his watch. Five o'clock. If he left now, he might catch the last bits of daylight. And if he reached the road and the conditions worsened, he wasn't too far away to turn back. He could grab his blanket and make himself an igloo shelter. He had done it once in Boy Scouts and although he hadn't spent the night inside the snow sculpture, he remembered it being warmer than it was outside. He checked his phone one more time. Still no signal.

Zach grabbed his sweatshirt from the backseat and put it on, pulled his hat down and his gloves up, and checked that his zipper was up to the top of his jacket. He opened his door and pulled himself up and out. He wanted to see around that bend in the road. He needed to know if anyone was coming.

"Come on, Skye." He held the door open and motioned for the dog to jump out. She glanced out the door and whined.

"Come on. We need to see if anyone's out there or if the plows have been through yet."

Skye hesitated. Finally, she obeyed and jumped out of the door and onto the snow. She gave Zach a quick nuzzle and started trotting back down the driveway to the cabin.

"Let's go." Zach gestured up the street to the main road. "There isn't anything back there for us."

Skye stood in place. She whimpered and glanced back the direction of the cabin again.

"No, Skye. We're going this way. We need to get to the main road and find help. There will be traffic. Maybe we can flag someone down."

The dog lowered her head and yowled, but she turned and reluctantly started out walking a step behind Zach. He looked back at Skye, feeling bad for the dog that he had grown up with.

The walk to the road looked completely different with the path covered in snow. But Zach knew this path by heart.

When he reached the main road, maybe he would have a cell signal. He would call his dad and he would be able to see if he had left Zach a message earlier. Anything so that he would know that his dad was safe. Any way for Zach to tell his dad that he, too, was safe. Despite what had happened to the cabin.

The path felt weird and quiet. Zach and Skye hadn't seen another living creature all afternoon. Usually there were squirrels, chipmunks, and sometimes raccoons. Today there was nothing.

Zach's thumb was still throbbing slightly, but he took that as a good sign. It meant his blood was still flowing—that he could still feel his fingers.

Zach glanced back at Skye, who was lapping up snow. She stopped what she was doing and stared at Zach. The snow was coming down so hard now that he could barely see Skye through the thick flakes.

"Come on, Skye."

They turned at the fork in the road and started on the narrower stretch. The trees engulfed them. They were almost a third of the way to the main road but would have no chance of getting a cell signal until they hit it. *No turning back now*, Zach thought, as he encouraged Skye forward.

Zach hunkered down into his coat. He probably looked like a turtle. Or maybe like a no-neck wrestler. The image made him laugh—a moment's release from the pain in his hand and the sleet that was slowly soaking through his clothes.

Zach tried to imagine what he and his dad would be doing if the blizzard hadn't hit their little cabin up north. They would come home with dirty gear and a couple of good fish stories.

They always exaggerated the size of the fish they caught. Zach's dad would say he caught a walleye that was *this big*. He would hold his hands eighteen inches apart, indicating the fish length. "No. Wait," he said. "It was actually *this big!*" The distance between hands would grow to two feet. Pretty soon that fish was over three feet long. "That was some big walleye." His dad's fish stories always made Zach laugh and his mom roll her eyes.

The sleet felt like it was coming down sideways now, the way it slapped Zach across the face. He wiped the wet slush away. He bent down to shield his face and grabbed the edge of his hat, forcing it further down so that it would be perfectly snug on his head.

When he got back to school, the first thing he would do would be compare his spring vacation in the frozen tundra to his friend Patrick's vacation in Hawaii. Zach would say, *True, you have a tan, but I have battle scars and frostbite. You don't have to be tough to get a tan. But frostbite—only the toughest guys survive frostbite.*

The main road was finally in sight. He looked back for Skye. She was struggling through the deep snow, limping slightly on her bad paw. And Zach didn't feel like he was doing much better as he trudged through the thick, wet layer toward the open expanse.

When Zach got closer to the main road, all he saw was white snow. Not a promising sign. Skye whined. The dog was clearly exhausted and she was coated with a thick, sticky layer of snow. Zach bent over to brush some of the snow off Skye and to catch his own breath. The cold air stabbed his lungs. The main road didn't look plowed like he'd hoped it would be.

Drifting snow had partially covered the place where the side road and the main road linked up and it looked like white sand dunes blocked his path. A cold, white desert extended as far as the eye could see.

His feet were sinking into deep snow every few feet. It took all the energy he had to keep moving. Was it worth it to try to go farther down the road? With every step more snow sneaked into his hiking boots. Zach dug the snow out as much as he could without removing the boots. The snow wet his socks and now the socks were freezing up. It felt like his feet were frozen in heavy ice blocks. Zach was slowing down and close to giving up.

On the main road, Zach was exposed to the wind with no shelter. The cold blew through his pants, making his legs ache. "Okay, Skye. Next time remind me to bring snow pants."

Skye perked up at the sound of her name and wagged her tail, but Zach's legs were freezing as the wet fabric clung to his skin. He needed to rest. He knew that if he sat down there would be a good chance he wouldn't be able to get up again, but he was so tired. So cold. He just wanted a little break.

The wind died down for a moment, and something caught his eye up the road. The wind and blowing snow had made it harder for Zach to see before, but now Zach could see a flash of red along the side of the road. Yes, definitely something red. Red—like his dad's car.

8

A jolt of excitement flashed through Zach, which turned almost immediately to fear as he realized that the car wasn't moving.

"Skye! Come on!" Zach yelled into the wind. He ran toward the car. Its hood dunked into the ditch at the side of the road. A figure inside was barely visible. And it was completely still. The body was slumped over the steering wheel.

Running through the snow drifts was like running on sand, but worse. He could barely move. Zach sunk into the snow with every step. The snow came up to Skye's belly, so she had to keep jumping over the snow to get through it. But they both knew they needed to get to the car.

The nose of the car was in the ditch, which left the tail end of the car sticking up. It was definitely his dad's car. He drove an older model sedan that Zach's mom had always hated. But his dad liked those old cars, so he refused to upgrade as long as the car still ran well.

"Dad! Dad!" Zach waded through the snow, which was waist-high in areas. Once he had plodded through the snowdrift, he wiped the driver's side window with his gloved hand, keeping the injured hand tucked inside his pocket.

His dad was still inside. How long had he been here? Five hours? Six hours? Had he been stranded here that long? Stuck in the snow so close that he could have walked to the cabin in good weather.

Zach cupped a hand up to the window and looked inside to see more clearly. His dad's eyes were closed. Was that blood on his forehead? His dad lay there asleep, or unconscious, or—Zach didn't want to finish that thought. He pounded on the window. "Dad! Wake up! Dad!"

His dad's eyes fluttered open. He slowly turned his head toward the window.

"Zach. Zach? Is that you?" His voice was muffled by the closed window.

"I'm here, Dad. I'm here. I'm going to get you out."

Skye barked and paced along the snowdrift behind Zach.

Zach whipped out his phone. No bars. Still no signal. *Unbelievable.*

Zach ran up to the road again, looking for help from anyone, but no cars passed. Nothing in either direction. He hadn't seen any vehicles on the road even as he was making his own way up to the cabin hours ago. Zach didn't expect the same kind of traffic that left them jammed in a long line of cars for hours during their summer commutes up north, but still. Where were the salt trucks and the snowplows? They should have been equipped to handle this kind of storm. If this had happened in the cities, the trucks would have gotten out right away. But this was far up north—in no-man's-land. There was no way of knowing when the plows would come through.

Zach rushed back to the car window.

"Dad," he yelled through the window. "Can you open the door?" Zach's dad reached for the handle, but as he moved his face turned a pale shade of gray and his eyes squeezed shut.

"Dad!"

He reached up to touch his shoulder and groaned, a pained look on his face. "My shoulder." He wore his seatbelt, but he had still hurt his shoulder when the car went off the road.

"Dad, don't try to move. I'll get the door open."

"My leg."

"What?"

"My leg is hurt, too—it's pretty bad."

Zach looked toward his dad's leg, but it was dark inside the car. The glass fogged up where he cupped his hand against the window and stared through. He looked at his dad lying there, helpless.

"Okay," Zach said. "Don't worry. I'll get you out of there."

Zach tried the door handle. Sleet had accumulated, sticking the door closed. Zach brushed the icy sheet away and pulled on the silver handle one more time. The door fell open, as gravity took control. *Well*, Zach thought, *there's one advantage of the car leaning forward, nose first, in a ditch.*

With the door open, Zach studied his dad's leg. A bone in the upper leg was broken and visible. Zach saw the white poking out from a tear in the pant leg. He turned away and puked.

He definitely wasn't expecting that. He grabbed a handful of snow and wiped it across his face. He took a deep breath before turning back to look at his dad.

"I don't think I can walk." His dad was probably right.

"I tried calling for help, but I can't get a signal."

"Zach, I'm sorry. I should have listened to the forecast."

"Don't worry, Dad. It will be alright."
Guilt was creeping through Zach. *He* had
been the one who'd insisted they go on this
stupid trip. *He* had gotten them into all
of this.

And now *he* would have to be the one to get
them out. "I'll be right back," Zach said and
scrambled back the way he came.

He hurried down the road back to his
car. Skye followed his every move. He
reached into the backseat for any supplies
that would help them. Zach grabbed the
blanket, the map, the tarp, the rope,
and the bungee cords. He also took the
remaining can of beans and the candy
bar. Zach hesitated with his hand near the
bear spray. He picked up the bottle, but
its contents were frozen solid. It wouldn't
do much good against a bear unless Zach
used it as a projectile. *It's just as well*, Zach
thought, *Dad is probably right, it's just for
scared tourists anyway*. He closed the car door.
His pocketknife and matches were still in his
pockets, but nothing else that was gathered

in the back seat seemed like it would be useful. He tied the map, bungee cords, beans, and candy bar up in the blanket and flung it in a pile on top of the tarp and rope.

Now he had to figure out how to move his dad. He needed to find something to make the frame of a sled with. Zach ran as fast as he could through the forest, searching until he found two branches that were at least four or five feet long and straight. The branches were sturdy enough that they wouldn't break under the weight of a body—at least he hoped they wouldn't. "Perfect."

Zach laid the branches on the ground parallel and about two feet apart. He set the tarp on top of the wood and tied everything together. He hoped it would support the weight of his dad so he could move him to a better location.

Zach looked around. It was already darker now than it had been when he left his dad's red car. How long had he been away from his dad? He glanced down at his watch and it was already 6:05. Zach pulled the makeshift sled behind him as he hurried through the woods to get back to his dad. He used both hands to move faster even though that meant he was exposing his injured hand to the blizzard.

What if his dad were unconscious? Zach had to hurry.

9

When Zach got to the open car door, his dad was still grimacing in pain.

"Dad," Zach said, gently tapping him on his good shoulder.

His dad turned to look at him. "It hurts."

The temperature was dropping fast now that dusk was upon them. Zach had heard something about staying in your car if you had an accident in bad weather, but his dad's car was tilted forward so it wouldn't be safe for them to sit inside. They couldn't go back to Zach's car either because it was sitting in the middle of the road. It would get covered in snow and if a plow finally came down it would slam right into them. Zach was certain that they couldn't survive another disaster like that.

They needed someplace that was warm and dry for the night, especially considering the shape his dad was in. He was already shivering and his lips had started turning purple. There was no way Zach's dad would make it through the night like this. They needed to find some place to get warm.

"We need to get you out of here. I'm going to undo the seatbelt."

Zach reached around his dad and found the seatbelt latch on his right side. The car moved a little. Zach stopped for a moment. He would have to be careful not to push the car any further in the ditch or he might risk injuring his dad even more. He slowly reached in again and pushed the latch release and the belt unhooked. In the process, he bumped into his dad's shoulder.

"Oh!"

The car creaked and moved again. This time it wobbled and slid a little bit further down in the ditch.

"Sorry!" Zach immediately drew back, afraid to touch the car now that it had actually moved.

He had never seen his dad so helpless and injured like this. His leg was badly hurt, he winced every time Zach came near his shoulder, and blood was matted on his face from a one-inch gash on his forehead.

"My leg jammed . . . into the dash . . ."

His face looked pained. Crinkles formed next to his eyes as he squeezed them shut. It was killing Zach to see his dad this way.

"Here. Wrap your arm around my shoulder." Zach reached in the car and grabbed his dad around the middle. "On three. One . . . two . . . three!" Zach pulled him out of the car as gently as possible. His dad tensed and cried out in agony but Zach knew that he didn't have time to stop. He pulled his dad the rest of the way out of the car and onto the snow bank. The car squeaked and wheezed. It rocked forward and rolled the rest of the way into the ditch. Skye, who had been sitting by the sled, jumped up and barked.

Zach helped his dad ease onto the tarp sled he had made.

"We're going to pull you out of here, just like riding a sled."

Zach was trying to sound positive, but it was difficult listening to his dad groan in pain.

Zach grabbed one of the bungee cords out of his blanket sack and started to attach it to the sled when Skye grabbed the cord with her teeth.

"Do you want to help?" Zach almost cried with relief. Skye grabbed the rope in her mouth and started to pull. It was slowly moving, but Skye was clearly pulling Zach's dad along.

"Hold on, girl," Zach grabbed the dog's collar. "Let's make this a little easier for you." Zach pulled out another bungee cord and wrapped it into a makeshift harness around Skye's shoulders. He attached the remaining bungee cords to the sled and picked up the rest of the supplies.

With his dad resting safely on the sled, Zach set out to find somewhere for them to wait out the storm overnight. It had become pretty clear to him that no one would be driving past them in this weather.

"Looks like you learned something useful in Cub Scouts," his dad said.

They both smiled, but neither of them said anything else. Zach pressed on, trying his best to keep Skye slow and steady as she pulled his dad behind her. He felt suddenly more like an adult than he ever had. He needed to take charge to get them out of this mess—for his dad.

"It's getting dark," his dad said.

Zach didn't answer at first. Then he said, "I know. We need to get out of the cold. Someplace we can stay for the night. I'm taking us deeper into the woods. I once saw a rocky ledge a ways from the cabin. I'm looking over there."

Skye trotted beside Zach. Every few steps she looked up at him to make sure he was still there.

Zach trudged through the snow. They had to turn to bypass mulberry bushes and fallen trees and the snow was getting deeper the farther into the woods they went.

Soon Skye was out of breath and limping along on her bad paw. The sled's weight was too much for the dog. Zach unhooked the sled from Skye's harness and attached it to his own belt loops. He set the blanket pack down at his dad's feet and started to pull.

"Good girl, Skye. Now how about I give it a try?" The dog barked appreciatively and ran a few steps ahead, leading their group on.

Pulling the sled reminded Zach of pulling the team equipment for football. They used a pull sled to work the chest muscles and build upper body strength. Coach would add more weights when you were ready. His dad's weight was actually less than what Zach pulled in football, but his dad was more fragile. In football, if Zach hit a bump nothing happened, but here his dad could be thrown off the sled.

"Keep going. You're doing great," Zach heard his coach in his mind.

"Stay with me, Dad. We're going to get through this."

Zach glanced back. His dad groaned from the sled, but mostly kept still. Zach looked ahead and steered them toward a rocky embankment. There might be something beyond the curve that would at least shelter them from the wind.

"This isn't exactly what we had planned, is it?"

"Nope," Zach said. He was trying to sound brave, but he didn't feel brave at all. He couldn't feel parts of his hand and face. He still didn't know if they would find shelter, but he kept pulling. The pulling gave him something to focus on.

His dad groaned as they covered increasingly rocky ground.

"I've got you." Zach steadied the sled. "Thought we'd be cleaning off some trout right about now."

"Naw. We would have thrown them back. I would have caught them all and you would have said, 'Let's go for pizza.'"

"Or else *I* would have caught them all."

"Right." They laughed.

"Oh." His dad grabbed his shoulder. "Hey, kid. Don't make me laugh, okay?"

"Okay," Zach said. "I'll try being less funny."

The blowing wind bit at Zach's cheeks. "We need to get out of this wind or we'll freeze to death. I think I remember a spot where we can spend the night," Zach yelled over the blowing wind. "Over into those woods. There's a high ridge in there. It'll at least shield us from this wind."

They were about two miles from where they had left his dad's now-totaled car. The woods were starting to look the same. Only a sliver of the sun hung low over the horizon. Zach blinked back tears. They needed shelter fast.

10

Zach didn't know how much farther he could pull the sled. His shoulders ached, his neck, his back. Not to mention he could barely feel his hands or his feet. His dad had grown quiet. "Dad! Stay with me!"

His dad stirred and grumbled. At least he was still alive.

Zach glanced back at Skye. She limped behind them now, hanging her head low. Zach didn't know how much farther he could go on. He was close to giving up hope that they would find anything when a hill appeared ahead. Zach gave a great heave to bring the sled forward as he climbed the hill, hoping he would be able to find some sort of shelter from the cold at the top.

Beyond the ridge, the rocky walls were indented as the shape of the rock took on the ridges of the land. Zach pulled his dad along, following the contours of the ridge. Around the next bend, he found an opening in the rocks.

The cave opening was an oddly shaped triangle. What little light there was left of the sun made it a few feet inside the cave entrance, and then it tapered off and dimmed until it all but vanished into the completely pitch-black distance. The cave would be warmer than staying outside and it did block the wind, which would be a relief. Zach didn't know if his hands and feet could survive another moment in the bitter wind.

"Here." Zach pulled the sled to one side of the cave. "Try and sit up if you can. Slowly."

Zach offered his arm and shoulder to his dad in case he needed to lean on something. He clutched Zach's arm and pushed himself up.

Zach noticed that his dad winced in pain every time he moved his leg the slightest bit.

Zach was in pain, too, but his was the pain of his hands and feet coming back to life. They tingled with the awful pins and needles of feeling coming back into the extremities. But he wanted to help his dad, which meant taking off his gloves.

Zach's dad reached up to his forehead. He was badly bruised, but the bleeding had stopped.

"You hit your head on something," Zach said. "Your leg is bad too. I'm going to try to stop the bleeding." Zach's fingers were stiff and difficult to move from the cold, but he cut off another long strip of his t-shirt and tied it around his dad's leg just above where the leg was broken. Zach tried not to look at the actual break or the bone. He knotted the strip and pulled the cloth tight, hoping it would at least partly secure the leg.

His dad was sweating and clenching his jaw. Zach felt his dad's forehead. It was definitely hot. He needed a doctor.

"The plows should come through by tomorrow," Zach said, trying to reassure his dad and also calm himself. "In the morning, I can make my way back to the road and get help." He grabbed his blanket-pack, emptied the contents, and threw the blanket over his dad. "For now, this blanket should help keep you warm," he told his dad.

Skye whimpered. Zach gave her a gentle look to get her to be quiet.

"We need to get you something to eat," Zach said, turning back to look at his dad. He fished his pocketknife out of his jeans. He would be extra careful using it this time. He took the can of beans from where he dropped it on the floor and started working the opener tool around it.

Zach scooped up some beans and held them to his dad's mouth.

His dad chewed slowly, working the cold beans down to a paste.

Zach smiled. He scooped some more beans from the can and fed them to his dad.

"Your hand. What happened?" his dad asked.

"Can opener accident." Zach shook his head. "It's nothing."

To think before he was so worried about having a great final hurrah for spring break! Now he just hoped they would make it out alive. He didn't think they would if they didn't heat up soon.

Suddenly, Zach remembered the matches in his pocket. He pulled them out and showed his dad. "I can make a fire. I just need something to burn." With new hope, Zach shoved the can of beans into his dad's lap, pulled back on his gloves, and bounded out of the cave.

"Where are you going?" Zach heard his dad yell, but Zach was already outside and back in the snowstorm. Skye started to follow him. "Stay here, Skye. You need to rest too."

Near the cave, Zach grabbed some twigs. He broke some small braches off the birch trees right outside the cave entrance. By now the sky was pitch dark, but the white that covered everything made the woods glow. The wind whirled up like a mini tornado taking off. Zach held up a hand to shield his face.

He gathered the sticks in his arms, as many as he could carry at once. He shook the snow off the branches as much as possible. Then he grabbed a few spruce branches with needles. They would be good for kindling to get the fire started. Zach brought them back into the cave and dropped them down. But he knew that he would need more and braced himself for a second trip out into the wind.

He really needed a thick chunk of wood or the fire would burn out right away. Zach wandered around, but kept a close eye on the cave. He didn't need to get lost alone in the woods. After a while, he found a fallen tree. He kicked at the wood and a piece of the trunk broke loose. The piece was nearly three feet long, but without an ax he couldn't chop it apart. And beggars can't be choosers, as his dad would say. Zach dragged the big log into the cave, satisfied that, if properly tended, the long piece would burn through the night.

Inside the cave, Zach gathered up the load of firewood and dragged the pile near his dad. They could burn the thick sticks

Zach had made the sled out of, but that would be a last resort. They might need the sled if Zach had to transport his dad back out of here tomorrow.

Zach set up the fire near the cave entrance for ventilation. He put the long piece of wood in place first: the base. Then he angled the smaller branches against the base so they met in the middle, the way he would have made a bonfire back home. He took the matches out of his pocket. The first two wouldn't light. "Come on. Come on!"

He struck the third match and it fizzled out too. Was the whole pack worthless? There were seven matches left. Zach tore off another one and set it between the matchbook covers and pulled. *Fsssst!*

The satisfying igniting sound came.

Zach held the match against the twigs, as close to the base as possible. It lit the small twigs but then smoked and died out right away. "Dang it!" He glanced at his dad lying there helpless and Skye sitting right by his side, shivering. Zach had to make this work.

He remembered the map. They didn't need it now. No one would be driving anywhere. Zach ripped the map into pieces and crumpled them into balls. He placed three wads of paper among the twigs and along the base log. Then he struck another match and lit the map pieces. They caught fire right away and soon the twigs beside them were starting to burn too. After a bit, the log lit up. Zach rubbed his hands together and then held them over the fire. It was warming up their small area of the cave. The relief swept over Zach with the warmth of the fire. He looked around at his dad and Skye. They too looked a little better. Skye had stopped shivering and some of the color was coming back into his dad's face. It was almost as if the three of them were sitting around the fire on a normal trip to the cabin.

Zach removed his hiking boots and set them near the fire to dry off.

He picked up a long, straight stick and started peeling off the tiny branches and leaves. This would make a good walking stick. His stomach growled. Or marshmallow roaster. That was one of the first things he would do when he got home—make s'mores. He flicked open the pocket knife and whittled away at the stick. The wood shavings came off easily. Pretty soon a small pile of shavings grew on the ground. His dad was nodding off while Zach worked.

"Dad! Dad, we have to stay awake. You probably have a concussion and hypothermia. If you fall asleep now you might not wake up."

His dad stirred and opened his eyes.

It was midnight.

Once the sun came up, Zach would go back to the road and flag down help.

Skye barked.

"Hush, Skye."

But she wouldn't stop barking. Zach immediately tensed up.

"What's wrong?"

Something was out there.

Skye bared her teeth. Her barking echoed off the cave walls.

"Hello? Who's there? Is someone there?" Zach grabbed the partially whittled stick and held it over his head, ready to strike. The hair on the back of his neck tingled. His heart hammered in his chest.

He heard a low growl coming from the mouth of the cave.

Skye kept barking. She was crouched down and ready to pounce on whatever was coming their way. At the sound of the growl she rushed forward, placing herself between Zach and the opening to the cave. Zach reached down to grab Skye's collar but she barked and jumped out of reach.

The fire crackled. Light from the flames cast a dancing shadow on the cave wall.

The shadowy figure at the cave's entrance grew larger, flickering ominously in the firelight. Zach stepped backward and tripped over his hiking boots, falling to the ground next to his dad.

"What is it?" Zach's dad groaned, barely conscious.

"I'm not sure. An animal . . . "

Simultaneously, they both saw the shadowy claw in the air. A big, black bear claw.

"It's a bear! Get some fire!" Zach's dad yelled. "The flames will scare it."

Zach jumped up and grabbed one of the branches from the fire. He waved it in the air and held it out as far as his arm would reach. His hand shook, casting a wavering light along the cave wall. Skye edged toward the cave opening.

A bear, almost bigger than the cave entrance itself, blocked their only way out. It growled, baring its teeth, then reared up on its hind legs when it saw them. Zach reached his fiery torch toward the bear.

The bear growled and swatted at the branch.

"Get out!" Zach yelled. He waved the branch just out of reach of the bear's paw. The claws, illuminated by the flames, looked like knives.

The bear was a lot scarier up close. Rising on its hind legs, it was about a foot taller than Zach. Why had the bear come into the cave? Had they stumbled on the bear's home? Weren't bears supposed to be hibernating this time of year?

Zach's hand shook. He held the torch as steadily as he could. His legs wobbled. He stared at the bear's sharp teeth.

The bear roared again and threw its head back. Skye lunged toward the bear, growling and snarling. It swatted at Skye's nose. She reared up just like the bear, but the bear towered over the dog.

"Skye, no! Skye!"

Skye stayed between Zach and the bear, continuing to growl and snarl. And Zach stayed between Skye and his dad, yelling and waving the flame.

Skye kept rotating with the bear as if they were prize fighters in a ring, her barks echoing off the cave walls.

When the bear got close to Zach, he swatted the torch in the bear's face and it growled. Zach stood his ground, keeping in front of his dad and held the torch firmly up to the bear. Zach waved his arms and yelled. The bear reared up one more time. Skye lunged and bit its leg. The bear yelped. It dropped down on its paws and lumbered out of the cave.

Zach shook violently. He'd never been so scared in his life. They had made it through two car accidents and a snowstorm only to face down a bear. He didn't know how much more he could take. He threw the burning torch back into the fire and sunk down to the ground.

Skye ambled toward Zach. She dropped at Zach's feet, exhausted.

"You did it, Skye. You scared him off. Good dog."

Zach rubbed Skye's neck, but he felt something wet. Blood.

"Skye, you're hurt." Zach suddenly remembered his phone had a flashlight. The cell didn't have service, but that didn't mean he couldn't use the flashlight feature. He shined the light over Skye's neck. "Where is it, Skye? Where does it hurt?" Zach ran his fingers through Skye's thick fur. Where was the blood coming from?

Then he found the source: cuts from the bear's claws swiping Skye's face and back. Skye had stopped the bear from killing them, but at what cost?

12

Zach woke with a start when he felt his dad shiver. Zach was confused, but one quick glance around the cave reminded him of the night's terrors and he turned to his dad.

"I'm here," Zach said.

"I'm so cold," his dad said. He was shaking the way people who are cold do, but he was sweating too. Morning light was streaming through the cave's entrance and Zach shifted out of the way so that he could use the sunlight to look into his dad's face, then on his leg. He pulled the cloth bandage back to see the wound. It was red. Zach touched the warm skin around the break.

"Ah!" his dad breathed fast through clenched teeth.

Zach had never felt so helpless in his life. He glanced at his watch. 8:23 a.m. They had spent the whole night in the cave. Skye lay at his feet, keeping them warm, but Zach knew they needed help soon. His whole body was stiff and cold.

At some point during the night the fire had gone out and the charred remains sat cold by the cave entrance.

"Your leg might be infected," Zach said. "We need to get you to a doctor in case you need antibiotics. I need to go for help."

Zach looked over himself. The cut on his hand had stopped bleeding, but both hands felt frostbitten and numb in places. He *also* needed a doctor.

He checked his hiking boots. The fire had dried them earlier, but Zach's feet had already suffered damage from the cold and ice inside his boots. He didn't know how far he could make it on his sore and frozen feet.

But if they stayed in the cave, no one would find them. No one would even know they were missing until it was too late.

Skye limped over and licked Zach's hand. Zach rubbed Skye's head.

"Skye, you need to stay here and stick with Dad in case that bear comes back. You stay."

Skye cocked her head to the side and whined.

"Sit, Skye."

Skye sat down. The slash mark from the bear had dried blood on it.

"Good girl." Zach patted Skye's head. "You stay with Dad. Skye, stay." Zach pulled on his hiking boots. They were cold but at least they were dry.

"Dad, I'm going to get help. I'll be back as soon as I can. Here's something to eat in case you get hungry." Zach tucked the candy bar into his dad's hand.

Zach stepped out of the cave. He could feel the chill of the air outside the cave hit him, but the snow had stopped falling. Zach looked around, trying to remember landmarks from the night before, but he couldn't remember much of anything besides the blinding snow. He had no idea what way he needed to go to find his way back to the road, but he had to at least try to get there. His dad needed help, and soon.

13

Zach checked his phone again for a signal. The screen was black. He pressed the power button and nothing happened. The phone had shut down. He stuffed it into his jacket pocket. He wouldn't be able to use it to reach anyone—9-1-1, his mom, any of the local stores. He would have to get by without it.

Zach shuffled along through the fresh powder, trying not to get snow inside his boots. Going through the snow was definitely easier without the heavy sled behind him but his legs still ached from yesterday's work and felt numb from the cold. He couldn't believe they had ended up in this situation: no working cars, Skye limping and hurt from fighting off a bear, his dad shivering in a cave with life-threatening injuries. Zach had a sick feeling in his stomach.

Snow had blown over the trail they had carved on their way to the cave. He brushed off the snow to see if he could retrace their steps from the previous day and found the remains of a faint path where he had pulled the heavy sled. At least it was something to start with.

A hawk circled overhead. A squirrel ran up a tree. It looked like he carried a nut in his mouth. If Zach ran into that bear again, he didn't have anything to protect himself with this time. Zach picked up his pace.

It was getting harder and harder to see their tracks from the night before. Which way should he go? He stopped at a fork in the path. Both the left and right routes had what looked like a track carved into the snow. One side had a few broken branches on a birch tree. It could have been from another animal, maybe even the bear, but Zach thought it was more likely that the broken branches were from when he had pushed through the trees to get to the cave. Zach stared at the two options. He had no idea what to do.

Well I have to do something, I don't think Dad has time to wait while I decide, Zach thought. But another nagging voice in his head reminded him that his dad also didn't have time to wait if Zach chose the wrong path. Zach chose the path with the broken branches. He hoped he wasn't following the broken branches straight to a bear. He didn't think he'd get off so easy if he met the bear again. Now he wished he had brought that bear spray with him. It was probably useless, but it was better than nothing.

Soon he started recognizing the path. He had chosen correctly. He hadn't realized it, but he had been holding his breath, afraid that at every turn he would realize he had been mistaken.

When Zach reached the road, the first thing he saw was his dad's car, dipping down into the ditch right where they had left it. The car was covered with more snow, but the road—the road was plowed! He sighed with relief. That meant someone had been through there. Would they be by again? How long ago had that been?

He looked both directions down the road. Should he wait for a car to pass or make his way to the next town? If he chose wrong, he might never run into anyone and his dad could die. Or he could die right out there on the road. The thought made his heart jump into his throat.

He slogged down the path toward his dad's tipped car. That was the direction of the nearest town.

A buzzing sound, like a chainsaw cutting logs, came from a ways away.

When Zach looked in the direction of the noise, he was blinded by the sun reflecting off his white surroundings. But the odd chainsaw sound grew louder. Then, out of the white, something moved. Something was coming down along the ditch on the opposite side of the road.

Zach waved his arms. The snow and the sun made him squint and almost completely close his eyes. The noise grew louder. A snowmobiler!

14

"**H**ey! Over here!" Zach yelled. He waved his arms. "I'm here!"

It didn't look like the rider had seen him, and he would never be able to hear Zach yelling over the loud engine.

Zach ran up out of the ditch and into the middle of the road, waving his arms and continuing to yell.

Zach's heart raced. Puffs of white smoke shot out of his mouth. "Wait! Help!"

The driver skidded to a stop in front of Zach. Snow shot out from beneath the sled skis.

The driver sat for a moment, staring at

Zach. Zach couldn't even see his eyes behind the tinted helmet glass.

Zach waved again and took a few steps toward the snowmobiler.

The rider removed his helmet. Or rather, *her* helmet. Long brown hair fell over her shoulders. She held the helmet in her arms.

"Are you alright?" she asked.

"My dad's hurt. He's in a cave. We need to get help!"

"Wait, slow down. What?"

"We need help! My cell phone died and my dad—my dad. And my dog. And there was a bear. Please!"

She whipped out a cell phone and dialed.

"Hi, my name is Emma Norton. We need an ambulance," she said into the phone. Then she looked around. "We're on the main road about five miles north of the junction to Bearclaw Lake."

Emma handed Zach her phone. The 9-1-1 operator shot off questions. Zach explained his dad's injuries and described where their cave shelter was as best as he could. The operator wanted to stay on the line, but Zach couldn't stand the thought of just waiting around, continuing to talk about how hurt his dad was. Zach let out a long breath and hung up. He thought that getting help would make him feel better but he felt more nervous now. What if they didn't get to his dad in time?

Emma's voice snapped him back to attention. "You're lucky you made it through that storm alive," she said. "Do you want me to bring you to your dad? I think I know the cave you were talking about. I used to play there as a kid."

Zach just nodded—no words would come out.

"Hold on," she said. Zach climbed on the back of the snowmobile and wrapped his arms around her waist. "I'm sorry I don't have an extra helmet." And they were off.

The cold wind slashed Zach's face. But he didn't care. All his attention was focused on making it back to the cave. He squinted his eyes most of the ride to shield them from the biting wind but also to stop the tears from rolling down his cheeks.

As they got closer, the red and blue flashing lights were already dancing against the white snow surrounding the cave.

Zach's heart pounded. His stomach did a somersault at the sight of the emergency responders. He had a horrible sinking feeling that they were too late.

15

As he hurried into the cave, Zach saw Skye lying with her head resting on his dad's chest, whimpering.

The paramedics leaned down next to his dad. One of them reached out for his dad's wrist.

A moment later, "We've got a pulse." As soon as the paramedics verified that, they sprang into action, doing a million things a minute. As they lifted his dad onto a stretcher and carried him to the ambulance, Zach followed the group with Emma by his side. He felt a surge of relief. His dad was alive . . . at least for now.

"I hope your dad's okay," Emma said.

"Me, too," Zach said. "Thanks for your help and for the ride."

"Glad to be of service," Emma replied, making a dramatic bow. She jumped back on her snowmobile and rode away.

Zach clambered into the ambulance with Skye at his heels. The paramedics looked at the dog, looked at each other, and shrugged. One of the paramedics lent him a phone so that Zach could call his mom. He knew she wouldn't pick up a call from a strange number. Still, he left her a message trying, and probably failing, to explain everything that had happened in the last twenty-four hours.

When they reached the hospital, one of the paramedics looked down at Skye again. "I know she rode with us, but you won't be allowed to take her into the hospital. Let me take her somewhere to get looked at. She seems like she could use some help too."

Zach wanted to keep Skye by his side, but he knew the paramedic was right. He nodded and the paramedic stayed outside with Skye as the rest of the group made their way into the hospital.

Zach followed his dad's stretcher down the hallway only to be stopped by the other paramedic. "Not so fast. We need to check you out for frostbite and that looks like a bad cut you've bandaged up."

Zach had no choice but to stay behind as he watched his dog sitting just past the automatic doors outside and his dad being carted away down a wide hallway.

The doctors verified that Zach had frostbite and started to warm up his hands and feet. As he regained circulation his skin turned pink and then white as angry, white blisters started to appear all over his left foot. The doctors drained the fluid from the blisters and wrapped up Zach's injuries. He would have to be on antibiotics to be sure he didn't get an infection, but given all that he had been through, Zach considered himself lucky. Besides, he was impatient to go see how his dad was.

While they stitched up his thumb, Zach was practically bouncing out of his seat. But when it was time to finally go to his dad's room, Zach was so scared he could barely move. He hobbled down the hallway on crutches and paused at his dad's door.

Zach took a deep breath and slowly entered the room. His dad looked horrible lying there in the hospital bed with an IV drip hanging from a rack at his side. His eyes were closed, but a large square bandage was taped to his forehead. Stubble dotted his chin. A sling covered his arm. Zach pulled up a chair that was against one wall and sat down next to the bed.

The doctor came in and reviewed a clipboard. "Are you the son?"

"Yes." Zach looked up. "Is he alright?"

"Your dad should be fine," the doctor said.

Zach breathed a sigh of relief.

"He was pretty banged up from that car accident, but it looks like we've got everything under control," the doctor said.

"Is he going to recover?"

"He should. His leg was infected, so we set the bone and have started him on antibiotics. He also has a broken collarbone. Probably hit the steering wheel. We gave him something for the pain. He needed a few stitches on his forehead and other than that we treated him for some mild hypothermia and frostbite." The doctor placed a hand on Zach's shoulder. "You saved his life, kid. You're a hero. Ever thought of being a paramedic?"

"Thanks," Zach said, suddenly embarrassed. "Uh, no. I want to study environmental science."

"Fair enough. Your survival skills will come in handy." The doctor folded his arms and looked at Zach. "Someone said you made a stretcher from some branches?"

"I'd call it more of a sled," Zach dipped his head in acknowledgement and chewed his bottom lip. "Where's Skye?"

"Who?" the doctor asked.

"Skye. Our dog."

"Oh, the dog. She's at the ranger station. Your dad will need to stay here for a few days, but the rangers said they could watch Skye till you can pick her up."

Zach breathed a sigh of relief.

"She had some pretty deep scratches on her face and back, they said."

"That was from a bear."

The doctor's eyebrows shot up. "A bear? Well, you had quite an adventure. You're lucky to be alive."

"I know," Zach said. "I know."

His dad's eyes fluttered open. Zach leaned over him. "Dad?"

"Zach? Zach, is that you?"

"Yeah, Dad. I'm here."

His dad seemed to give a half smile before his eyes closed again.

"He'll be in and out of consciousness for a while. The pain meds are going to make him groggy. He may not remember much of the next twenty-four to forty-eight hours. But you're welcome to wait in here if you'd like."

Zach had nowhere else to go. He had no car. Both cars were stuck out in the snow.

"I think we need a tow truck," he said. "Or two."

***

Zach slept most of the afternoon curled up in the hospital chair waiting. The doctor said his dad would be fine, but until Zach heard it from his own dad's mouth he wouldn't be satisfied.

Around five o'clock, Zach's dad woke up.

"Hey," Zach said.

His dad scanned the room. "Where am I?"

"The hospital, up north."

Zach's dad looked and groaned, "Ugh. So that wasn't a dream?"

"Unfortunately, no. You're pretty banged up. The doctor said you need to stay here for a few days."

"Oh, Zach. What about your spring break? I'm sorry. This was supposed to be our last hurrah."

Zach waved it off. "We're all safe. And we'll have a story to tell."

"Where's Skye?"

Zach exhaled. "She's at the ranger station.

They're watching her until we go home. She saved us from the bear."

His dad squinted. "She did?"

"Yep. She scared off the bear."

"Wow."

"Yep."

"And to think I thought we shouldn't bring her."

"I know," Zach said, laughing for the first time in what seemed like forever.

They both sat in silence for a few minutes, not sure what to say next.

"That storm was worse than they predicted," his dad said.

"The snowdrifts were *this big*," Zach held his hand a foot off the ground.

"No," his dad said. "*This big*!" His dad held his hand two feet off the ground.

"Actually," Zach said. "They were huge! They were *this big*!" Zach indicated snowdrifts that were almost up to his waist. "Enormous. The blizzard of the century."

"And we made it through." Then his dad turned serious. "I'm glad you're okay."

Zach felt himself smile. He had been scared, but they made it through. And now they had a great story to tell, no exaggeration necessary.

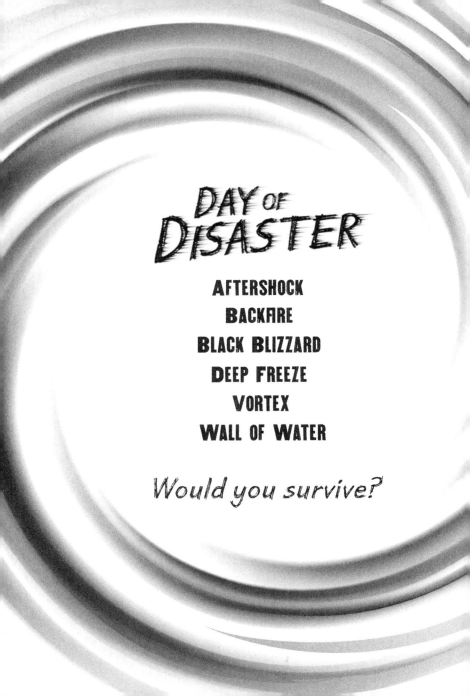

DAY OF DISASTER

AFTERSHOCK
BACKFIRE
BLACK BLIZZARD
DEEP FREEZE
VORTEX
WALL OF WATER

Would you survive?

SOME PLACES HOLD MORE SECRETS THAN PEOPLE.
ENTER AT YOUR OWN RISK.

THE ATLAS OF CURSED PLACES

BREAKDOWN

KATHRYN J. BEHERNS

THE ATLAS OF CURSED PLACES

DEADMAN ANCHOR

K.R. COLEMAN

THE ATLAS OF CURSED PLACES

DIRECTOR'S CUT

VANESSA ACTON

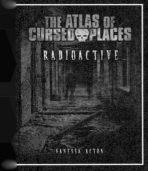

THE ATLAS OF CURSED PLACES

RADIOACTIVE

VANESSA ACTON

THE ATLAS OF CURSED PLACES

SKELETON TOWER

VANESSA ACTON

THE ATLAS OF CURSED PLACES

THE GATEWAY

KATHRYN J. BEHERNS

THE ATLAS OF CURSED PLACES

About the Author

Kristin F. Johnson lives in Minneapolis, Minnesota, and teaches writing at a local college. She spent two years as a media specialist and children's librarian in Minneapolis Public Schools. In 2013 and again in 2015, she won Minnesota State Arts Board Artist Initiative grants for her writing. She loves dogs and has a chocolate Labrador retriever.